God's Little Dreamer

ANN KIEMEL ANDERSON

Illustrations by Sandra Powell Lane

Harvest House Publishers
Eugene, Oregon 97402

To join THE DREAMER'S CLUB,
write to:

Ann Kiemel Anderson
c/o Harvest House Publishers
1075 Arrowsmith
Eugene, Oregon 97402

•

God's Little Dreamer

Copyright ©1990 by Harvest House Publishers
Eugene, Oregon 97402

Library of Congress Cataloging-in-Publication Data

Anderson, Ann Kiemel
God's little dreamer/Ann Kiemel Anderson.
p.   cm.
Summary: God gives Madison a dream that makes every day
magnificent for her.
ISBN 0-89081-785-5
[1. Christian life—Fiction.]   I. Title.
PZ7.A5197Go   1990

[E]—dc20   90-33475
                                                   CIP
                                                   AC

Printed in the United States of America.

To my four cherished sons—Taylor, Brock, Colson, and Brandt.

To every child courageous enough to embrace a dream and follow Jesus.

And in memory of my 82-year-old dad,
Harold Kiemel. He inspired the story. I was his Madison.

*I*t was a glorious fall day. Madison pressed her nose against the windowpane and watched the wind scuttle the leaves along the sidewalk.

She had a dozen freckles on her nose, and each freckle belonged to someone. Five were for her mommy to kiss. Six for her daddy. And one for her Grandma Jo.

Madison loved days like this. The sun was high...so high...in the sky that she had to squint her blue eyes when she looked up. She spun and twirled and danced with the garden rake through the leaves scattered in her yard. Then she stopped and raked them into tall towers. One, two, three, four towers covered the corners of her yard.

Madison ran with all her might and jumped on each tower. She pretended she was a long-lost princess climbing the walls to her very own castle.

G O D ' S   L I T T L E   D R E A M E R / 7

Suddenly someone picked her up and tossed her high in the air, leaves and all. She knew who it was.

"Oh, Dad! You just captured a princess!" said Madison when her feet were finally on the ground.

"A princess?" asked her dad. "I knew you were special, but I didn't know you were a princess."

Madison straightened her long brown braids. She tried to look dignified and grand like a princess should.

Madison's dad tweaked her nose and smiled at her. "You *are* special, Madison," he said. "God made every boy and every girl to have dreams in their hearts so they can grow up and do something great. Really great!"

"Dad, is having a dream like pretending I'm a princess and these leaves are the towers of my castle?"

He smiled. "Dreams are ideas, Madison. Ideas about things we can do and people we can love if we are brave enough and strong enough. You might not be a princess in a castle, but I know God has big plans for you!"

Madison's eyebrows frowned a little, the way they always did when she was thinking hard.

"My friend Anna plays with dolls and wants to be a mommy," she said slowly. "Taylor wants to drive a street sweeper when he grows up, and Brock wants to race motorcycles. Dad, is that what you're talking about?"

Madison's father walked over to the porch and sat down with her on the top step.

"There are many kinds of dreams, Madison—some are big and some are little, but every dream can change the world."

. . . .

"Dad," asked Madison, "what should my dream be? I want something special to dream about."

Madison's dad pulled a leaf out of her hair. "Ask God to give you a special dream, Madison. The dream God gives you will make you feel happy inside."

Madison sat very still, dreaming big dreams while her fingers twisted and tugged at one of her braids. Finally her dad stood up and said, "It's time to eat, Madison. Let's go inside."

That night Madison pulled her blankets up around her chin and thought about dreams. The friendly light of the moon spilled in through her window. It filled the room with its silver glow. As she drifted off to sleep, the moon seemed to say, "Don't worry, Madison, God has a dream *just* for you."

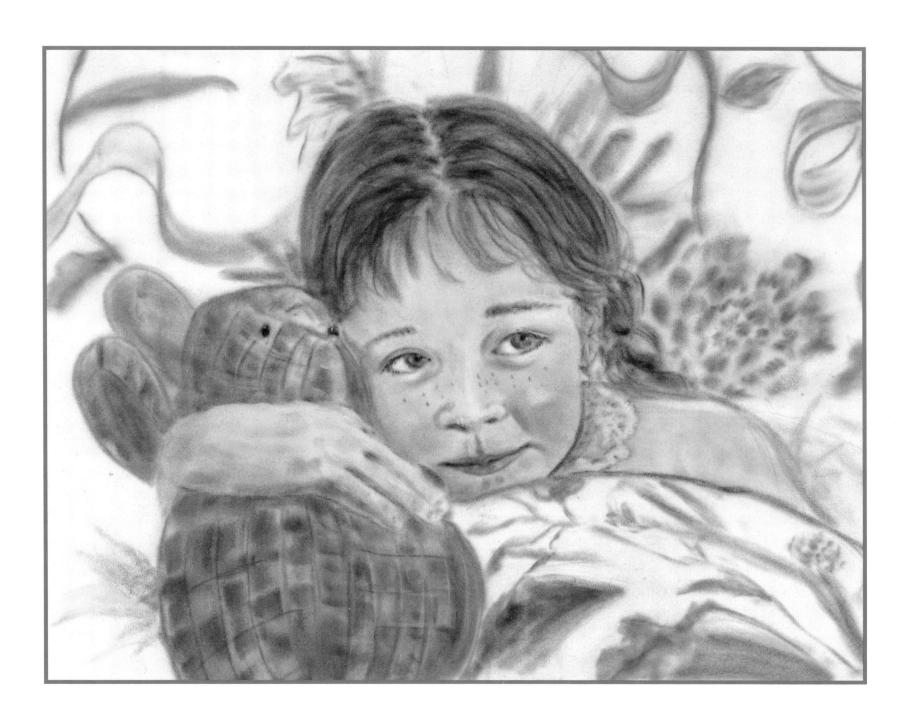

*T*he next day Madison hurried to finish her chores. "Bye, Mom," she called and skipped out the back door. She squeezed through a gap in the picket fence and knocked on the windowpane of Suzie's house.

"C'mon in!" Suzie shouted through the glass. "Want to color?"

Suzie could color so wonderfully. She always chose the right crayon and never colored outside the lines. "Maybe my special dream is to color like Suzie," thought Madison as she ran around to the front door.

GOD'S LITTLE DREAMER/19

Suzie and Madison were busy at the table when Suzie's big brother came clattering in. He dropped his jacket and baseball bat on the couch and headed for the fruit basket.

"Watcha doin'?" Benji asked between bites of a crunchy apple.

"We are artists," Suzie announced without looking up. She didn't want to mess up the circus clown she was coloring.

Benji watched for a minute. "Hey, why don't you two have a contest? I'll be the judge and pick the winner!"

Madison's eyes sparkled as she rummaged through the color box to find the blue-green crayon. She colored ever so carefully. She was sure that her picture would win.

When the pictures were finished, Benji looked closely at each one. Madison held her breath.

"Suzie wins," Benji announced.

Suzie smiled proudly, but Madison's face got very red. She wanted to throw the box of crayons and her coloring book across the room. She ran...very fast...out of Suzie's house. She would never color again. She cried all the way back to her house. Maybe dreams were too hard.

Madison almost ran into her dad as she burst through the door. "What's the matter, Madison?" he asked. Between sobs she told him about the contest.

Madison's father pulled her onto his lap and wrapped his big, strong arms around her. His hug helped her to stop shaking. He waited until she had stopped crying and then he said, "Madison, dreams cannot live in your heart if there are bad feelings growing inside. Just because your picture didn't win doesn't mean that it isn't a pretty picture, or that God doesn't love you just as much."

Madison sniffed a little and hugged her dad tight. Then she went into the bathroom and locked the door. She stood on tiptoe, looked into the mirror, and wiped away the tear streaks from her cheeks. "Madison," she said to herself, "you must let God help you find a dream."

Madison put on her coat and went outside to walk through the leaves on the sidewalk. "Why are dreams so hard?" she wondered. She wanted so very much to have her own special dream.

Madison had almost reached the end of the block when she saw Neil sitting at the curb, his chin resting on his knees. Neil was in her class at school, but she never talked to him. The other kids made fun of him. His ears stuck out and his thick glasses made his eyes look big.

Madison started to walk by, but then she stopped.

GOD'S LITTLE DREAMER/29

Neil looked so lonely. Madison walked slowly over to the curb and stood there for a minute. Then she plopped down next to Neil. "Hi," she said. Neil didn't answer.

Madison tried again. "My mom is baking cookies. They're still warm from the oven. Would you like to come over to my house?"

For a long time Neil didn't say anything. He just stared at her with his big, sad eyes. Madison stood up and held out her hand to Neil. This time he smiled back, and they walked to her house together.

*T*hat night Madison's father sat at the end of her bed and said, "Madison, I saw you do something today that was magnificent."

"*Magnificent?* What does that mean?" she asked.

"Magnificent is when God takes someone very simple...like you or me...and splashes sparkles all around and over their dreams...to make them big and great. To make them shine."

"Loving people, Madison, is the most magnificent dream of all."

"How can I do that, Dad?" asked Madison.

"You sit with someone at lunch if no one else does," Dad answered. "You play with them if they have no one to play with. You share your toys, your happy thoughts, and even your fears with them."

Madison thought about Neil and her eyes began to shine. She was only one, simple, little girl…with braids and a dozen freckles. But she and God could make a difference in the world.

Madison threw her arms around her dad. "Oh, Dad, with this dream EVERY DAY is magnificent!"

P.S. Hi. I'm Ann. I wrote this story.
Someday I will be old and gone, and I need you to
take my place to love the world for Jesus.
If you want to join *The Dreamer's Club,*
write to me, and I will send you a sticker.
We can dream together.